BUSY, BUSY MOUSE

by **VIRGINIA KROLL**

illustrated by **FUMI KOSAKA**

VIKING

VIKING

Published by the Penguin Group

Penguin Putnam Books for Young Readers, 345 Hudson Street,

New York, New York 10014, U.S.A.

Penguin Books Ltd, 80 Strand, London WC2R 0RL, England

Penguin Books Australia Ltd, 250 Camberwell Road, Camberwell, Victoria 3124, Australia

Penguin Books Canada Ltd, 10 Alcorn Avenue, Toronto, Ontario, Canada M4V 3B2

Penguin Books (N.Z.) Ltd, 182-190 Wairau Road, Auckland 10, New Zealand

Penguin Books Ltd, Registered Offices: Harmondsworth, Middlesex, England

First published in 2003 by Viking, a division of Penguin Putnam Books for Young Readers.

1 3 5 7 9 10 8 6 4 2

LIBRARY OF CONGRESS CATALOGING-IN-PUBLICATION DATA

Kroll, Virginia L.

Busy, busy mouse / by Virginia Kroll ; illustrated by Fumi Kosaka.

p. cm.

Summary: A mouse rests during the day while the family he lives with is
very busy, but when they go to sleep he is the one who has much to do.

ISBN 0-670-03527-0

[1. Mice—Fiction. 2. Stories in rhyme.] I. Kosaka, Fumi, ill. II.Title.

PZ8.3.K8997 Bu 2003   [E]—dc21   2002015551

Manufactured in China

Set in Clarendon

Book design by Teresa Kietlinski

With love to Father Walter Szczesny,

my busy, busy friend.

– V.K.

To Kyushu no Obachan,

who has always been there for me

and my family despite her busy life!

– F. K.

Up comes the sun.
Good morning, everyone.

Baby crying.
Eggs frying.

Clay smashing.
Blocks bashing.

Telephone ringing.
Canary singing.

Pictures scribbled.
Cookies nibbled.

All the day,
Eat, talk, play.

Busy, busy house . . .

Quiet, quiet mouse.

Down goes the sun.
Good evening, everyone.

Clay put back.

Blocks in a stack.

Canary fed.
Stories read.

Teeth brushed.
Baby hushed.

Off to bed,
You sleepyhead.

All the night,
Sleeping tight.
Quiet, quiet house . . .

Busy, busy mouse!